Tink and the Messy Mystery

~⋆ Book Two ⋆~

New York

Illustrated by the Disney Storybook Artists
Designed by Deborah Boone

Copyright © 2010 Disney Enterprises, Inc.
All rights reserved. Published by Disney Press, an imprint of Disney Book Group.
No part of this book may be reproduced or transmitted in any form or by any means,
electronic or mechanical, including photocopying, recording, or by any information
storage and retrieval system, without written permission from the publisher.
For information address Disney Press, 114 Fifth Avenue, New York, New York 10011-5690.

Printed in China

First Edition
1 3 5 7 9 10 8 6 4 2

Library of Congress Catalog Card Number on file.

ISBN 978-1-4231-2592-1
F904-9088-1-10136

For more Disney Press fun,
visit www.disneybooks.com

One morning, Tink arrived at her workshop and opened the door. "Oh, my!" she cried. The place was a mess! And someone had taken the set of measuring spoons the pots-and-pans fairy was mending.

Who would do such a thing? Tink wondered. "Maybe a baking-talent fairy needed the measuring spoons in a hurry," Tink said

Tink didn't mind about the mess, but she was worried about the spoons. "Those spoons aren't fixed yet. The pinch-of-this spoon dispenses a pinch of that. And the add-a-dab spoon is still adding a dollop. I'd better go to the kitchen and warn the baking talents," Tink said with determination.

When Tink arrived in the kitchen, she found Dulcie and the other baking-talent fairies in a tizzy.

"Someone's made a mess of the kitchen," Dulcie complained. "And that's not all. Three gingerbread cupcakes were stolen."

"Or eaten," Tink said. "Look at all those crumbs on the floor. Let's look in the tearoom. Whoever ate those cupcakes probably needed a cup of tea to wash them down."

Tink and Dulcie went into the tearoom. There, they found Prilla and Fira staring at another big mess!

"What happened here?" asked Tink.

"We don't know," Fira answered. "When we came in for breakfast, this is what we found!"

"Oh, no!" Dulcie cried. "The silver sugar shaker is missing!"

"Who is making all this mischief? And why?" wondered Prilla.

"I don't know," Tink answered. "But I'm going to find out. Dulcie, you and Fira stay here and keep watch in case the culprit comes back. Prilla, you and I will follow every clue, starting with this trail of sugar."

Tink and Prilla followed the trail of sugar out of the tearoom. It led them into the lobby and then up a circular staircase. Next, it brought the fairies through the branches of the Home Tree.

Finally, the trail stopped right at Beck's bedroom door.

Beck was an animal-talent fairy and one of Tink's very best friends.

The door to Beck's room was open, so Tink and Prilla peeked inside. Beck wasn't there . . . but the mixing spoons and the silver sugar shaker were!

"Do you think Beck could have made all those messes?" Prilla asked Tink.

"I know she wouldn't," Tink replied firmly. "There's a mystery here, and we need to solve it. Come on, let's investigate."

Tink and Prilla flew through Pixie Hollow, looking for clues. Before long, they spotted Beck—and she was behaving very strangely. She darted from one bush to another, as if she was hiding.

As Tink and Prilla watched, Beck darted into the art fairy Bess's studio.

"Why is Beck sneaking around like that?" Prilla wondered.

"I don't know," Tink answered with a frown. "Let's catch up and ask her."

But by the time Tink and Prilla got to Bess's studio, Beck was gone.

Just then, Bess flew up. "Oh, no!" she cried.

"Look at my studio! It's a mess. Even more than usual, I mean. And the cake I was painting is gone!"

Prilla turned to Tink. "The mess-making thief has struck again!" she whispered.

"Come on," said Tink. "We have to find Beck and find out what's going on."

Tink and Prilla finally spotted Beck in Lily's garden. They hid behind a flower and tried to decide what to do.

"How can you be sure that Beck isn't the mess-making thief?" Prilla whispered. "We saw her coming out of Bess's studio. She was right at the scene of the crime."

"Beck didn't have time to make such a mess in Bess's studio," Tink whispered back, "much less eat a whole cake!"

"Then what was she doing there?" Prilla wondered.

"I wish I knew," said Tink.

Just then, Beck sprang up behind them. "AH-HAH! Caught you!" she shouted. But when she saw Tink and Prilla, she blinked in surprise. "Tink? Prilla? What are you doing here?"

"Following you," Tink answered.

"Following me?" asked Beck. "Why?"

"Someone has been making messes all over Pixie Hollow," Tink told her.

"And the clues all point to you," Prilla added.

Beck looked surprised. Then she began to laugh. "You've been following me, and I've been following them," she said, pointing toward the bushes.

"Come out, you sillies. I see you!" Beck called. To Tink and Prilla's amazement, three baby hedgehogs came rolling out of the grass.

"We were supposed to be playing hide-and-seek," Beck explained. "But these rascals keep running away. I've been chasing them all morning, but they were always one step ahead of me. They're more than I can handle."

"Why didn't you ask us for help?" Tink said.

"I thought I could do it on my own," Beck replied with a sigh.

With help from Tink and Prilla, Beck built a little playpen for the hedgehogs.

"Now they can have fun . . . and you can keep track of them," Prilla told Beck.

"Well," said Tink, "it looks like the messy mystery is solved."